The Dig

By Patricia Turgeon

Illustrated by Sonja Wagenius

Lupine Hill
PUBLISHING

Library of Congress Control Number: 2023910856
ISBN 978-1-7374536-1-1 (paperback)

[1. Dinosaurs - Fiction. 2. Dream – Fiction.
3. Children 6 – 10 Fiction.
4. Children's Fiction.]

Printed by KDP
An Amazon.com Company

This book was typeset in Garamond Eb

Lupine Hill Publishing
Alexandria, MN

visit me at: www.patriciaturgeon.com

*This book is dedicated to
God, Who gave me the passion and
the gift to write. To Him be the glory.*

*And to Emily, James, David,
Daniel, and Henry*

P.T.

Chapter 1

"James, turn out the light," eight-year-old David whispered.

"In a minute," his ten-year-old brother answered.

"But I can't sleep. The light is too bright," David persisted.

"Alright," James answered reluctantly. He reached for the flashlight on his nightstand, turned out the light, and pulled a blanket over his head. "Is that better?"

"I guess," David answered, rolling over.

A few minutes later the door creaked open. "Bud, lights out," Mom whispered.

"Can't I read five more minutes?" he asked, peeking out from under the blanket. "Please?"

"It must be a good book," Mom replied, walking into the room holding two-year-old Henry.

"Yeah. It's about dinosaurs ... Mom, I

want to be a paleontologist when I grow up."

"A what?" thirteen-year-old Sarah asked joining them.

"Somebody who studies dinosaurs."

"Oh, that ... Guess what?"

"What?"

"Dad said we're finishing the fence tomorrow!"

"Maybe we can help dig the hole for the last post!" David exclaimed, sitting up in bed.

"We should dig to China!" six-year-old Daniel said, sitting up in his bed. "Henry, say 'China'."

"CHINA!" Henry replied enthusiastically.

Sarah giggled.

"China! China!" Daniel shouted, jumping up and down on his bed.

"CHINA! CHINA!" Henry repeated almost jumping out of his mother's arms.

"Okay, that's enough," Mom stated. "It's time for bed."

"Alright, but tomorrow I'm digging to ..."

"Daniel," Sarah interrupted, "Gramma was just teasing the other day when she asked if we were digging to China. It's not possible."

"I KNOW SARAH!" Daniel exclaimed,

"I'm just pretending."

"James, maybe we'll find a dinosaur bone!" David interjected.

"That's highly unlikely," Sarah retorted.

"She's right. I don't think any dinosaur bones have ever been found around here," James agreed.

"Well, maybe we'll be the first to find some!" David persisted.

"Maybe," James agreed smiling. He set down his book and sat up a little straighter. He could see the newspaper headline: LOCAL BOYS UNCOVER A DINOSAUR BONE.

"Guys, forget about dinosaurs!" Sarah declared, rolling her eyes. "We're getting our puppy soon!"

"Okay, time for bed," Mom firmly repeated. "Sweet dreams."

"James' dreams will be anything but sweet," Sarah stated, heading for the door. "He'll probably have nightmares with all the pizza he ate."

"That's enough, Sarah."

As James snuggled under the covers,

he heard the soft breathing of his brothers in their beds. They were already asleep. And with that, he closed his eyes and drifted off into a ... D.E.E.P...D.E.E.P... SLEEEEEEEP..............

Chapter 2

"James, breakfast!" Mom called up the stairs.

"Coming."

As he entered the sunny kitchen, his siblings Sarah, David, Daniel, and Henry were already eating their cheesy egg scramble and blueberry muffins.

"Morning, James," Dad smiled, looking up from his phone.

"Morning," he answered with a yawn.

"We're going to finish the fence today!" Sarah exclaimed with eyes sparkling. "We're getting our puppy in just two days!"

"Can I help?" James asked between

mouthfuls.

"Me too?" David inquired.

"Of course," Dad replied. "You can start digging the hole for the last post.

I'll be out after I finish my coffee."

"How deep?" James asked, carrying his plate to the sink and grabbing his cap.

"About 31 inches."

"China?!" Henry suggested.

"No." Sarah laughed.

James and David ran out the door, grabbed their shovels, and started to dig. It was a warm morning. Sweat was soon running down their faces, but that didn't stop them. Suddenly, they hit something.

"What was that?" David asked.

"I don't know," James answered. He carefully reached his gloved hand into the hole and pulled out a broken dish.

The siblings stared at each other and scrambled out of the dirt pile. "Dad! Mom!" they yelled, running into the kitchen.

"What did you find?" Dad asked. "Hmm … This plate looks old," he added, examining the broken object. "Look, it was made in Holland."

"That's cool," Mom said, looking up from the dishes.

"Come on, David. Let's see what else we can find!" James raced out the door.

"Save some treasure for me," Mom called after them. "I want to dig too!"

"Okay!"

"Wait for me!" Daniel exclaimed, jumping up from the table and grabbing his cap from the hook.

"Hey, Bud, what about your breakfast?" Mom asked.

"I'm done!"

"I'm coming too," Sarah stated, determined that the fence project would be completed so they could get the puppy.

"Sarah, would you take Henry with you?"

"Yes, Mom ... Come, Henry, let's go outside."

She lifted him out of the highchair and headed for the door. When they reached the dig site, James had just found something else.

"What is it?" David asked looking intently at the shovel.

"It looks like a chopstick," Sarah answered. The family had ordered Chinese takeout the other night and she had asked for chopsticks.

"China?!" Henry asked again – a little

more excited this time.

"No, Henry! Not China!!" Sarah exclaimed impatiently.

"I want to dig, too!" Daniel declared with hands on his hips.

"Okay," James replied, handing him the shovel.

Chapter 3

"Guys, the hole is big enough," Sarah reminded them a half-hour later. "We're just putting in a fence post."

The boys ignored her and continued to dig. The fence project was forgotten. They were looking for buried treasure. They found an old baseball, a porcelain cup with a painted pink rose, a cracked Frisbee, and ...

James was about to remove another load of dirt when the shovel hit something with a THUD. He tried in another spot and then another. The result was the same.

"Hmm, that's strange," he thought.

"Probably just a big rock," David suggested.

"I don't think so," he answered.

"What is it then?" the others asked, peering into the hole.

"China! China!" Henry declared, jumping up and down.

Daniel grinned. David shook his head. Sarah rolled her eyes.

"No, Henry," James replied seriously. "Dad! Mom! Come quick!"

"What do you need?" Dad answered from the back door.

"We found something!" James exclaimed. "It's BIG!!"

Dad grabbed his hat and gloves from the mudroom and walked outside to the dig site. He climbed into the hole and knelt on the dirt. With his gloved hand, he felt around the object. "Hmm, you're right, James. Whatever it is, it's really big,"

"What did you find?" Mom asked, walking up with a cup of coffee.

"Not sure," Dad answered, climbing out. "Boys, we need to make this hole bigger."

James, David, and Daniel were so excited they almost knocked each other over attempting to climb in. Watching from a distance, Henry looked over at his mom and shook his head.

"Silly boys," Mom said.

At that moment Dad's phone rang. "Oh, no! I forgot about my conference call!"

"On a Saturday?" James moaned.

"Sorry, Guys, but I have to take this." Dad walked toward the house. "Good morning, Mr....."

"Now what are we going to do?" David wondered.

"I don't know," James answered. "He'll be tied up for hours."

"I'll help!" Sarah interjected.

"You will?" James said surprised. "Thanks!"

"How come?" Daniel wondered out loud. His sister never had time for such stuff.

Sarah shrugged. Secretly she was wondering if they had uncovered the ruins of an ancient civilization or maybe it was a ....

"It's really warm," Mom commented. "I'll get your water bottles. Come, Henry, you can help."

"Put lots of ice in mine," David called after her.

"Can you bring some granola bars?" James asked. "I'm starving."

"Thanks, Mom," Sarah added.

"How are we ever going to get this out?" Daniel wondered as their mom and little brother headed toward the house.

"Like Dad said we have to make the hole bigger. Come on, we can do this." Sarah grabbed a shovel and began to dig. "Well, are you going to help me or just stand there?!"

"I'll get another shovel," David said, running toward the shed.

"I need one too!" Daniel added.

Within minutes, dirt was flying in all directions. "Hey, watch it!" said one.

"Sorry!" said another. And so it went …

Chapter 4

"**I**'m tired!" Daniel sat abruptly on a mound of dirt.

"Me too!" James and David agreed, joining him.

"Guys, you can't stop now!" Sarah wailed.

At that moment, Dad stuck his head out the back door. "How's it going?"

"Dad, we're so close to getting it out, but the boys won't help," Sarah answered.

"I'll be right out." A few minutes later, he was kneeling in the hole. "You've done a great job, Guys. Now we need to use the shovels as levers and pry it out."

Excited by the encouragement, the boys got up and grabbed their shovels.

"Lunch is ready!" Mom called from the back door. "Come and eat."

"Aw, Mom, not yet," David said.

"It can't be lunchtime already," Daniel

added. "We just ate breakfast."

"You've been out here for hours," Mom answered, walking up to the dig site with Henry following.

"Mom, we just need five more minutes," Sarah pleaded.

"Yeah. All we have to do is pry it out," James added hopefully.

"The kids are right," Dad said. "We're almost done."

"Alright," Mom agreed reluctantly, "but I have a surprise in the oven, and I don't want it to burn."

"You can go back in. We'll be right there," Dad assured her.

"And miss out on all the excitement? No way."

"Okay, Guys, dig your shovel into the ground right under the object. When I count to three, push down on the handle. Ready?"

They nodded.

"Okay ....one ... two ... three! PUSH!"

They pushed and the object moved slightly.

"Okay, this time push down harder," Dad directed. "One ... two ... three ... Push!"

The object was loose. With everyone working together, they carefully pulled it out of the hole and set it on the grass.

"What is it?" Daniel asked.

"It looks like a tree stump," Mom replied.

"James, get the garden hose," Dad instructed. "There's so much dirt on it, it's hard to tell."

"Yes, Dad."

"David, get the brush from the garage – the one I use to wash the car."

"Okay, Dad," David answered, running off.

A few minutes later, they were back. While James held the hose, Dad carefully scrubbed the object. "Okay, Bud, give it one final rinse," Dad said a short time later.

"What is it?" Daniel asked again.

"I think it's a bone," Dad answered, "and it appears to be in perfect condition."

"It's bigger than Henry," Mom thought, looking over at the two-year-old playing in the sandbox.

"James, I think ..." David began.

"It's a DINOSAUR BONE!"   Sarah

shrieked.

"Shh! Not so loud!" James whispered. "We don't want snoopy Mr. Baxter to

hear."

"James, that's not polite," Mom cautioned.

"But, Mom, it's true. He's always watching us with his binoculars."

"James, that's enough!" Dad warned.
"Sorry."

Mr. Baxter was a retired TV reporter who lived next door. He missed his reporting days and was always on the lookout for a big story.

He was just taking out his trash when the bone was discovered. He hobbled into the house, got out his binoculars, and peered out the window into the backyard next door. "Good work chaps!" he whispered, walking over to his phone.

Chapter 5

"**W**hat are we going to do with it?" Daniel wondered.

"Well, we can't leave it out here," James answered.

"I know that," Daniel said, "but what are we going to do with it?"

"I'm putting it in my room," James stated.

"You mean our room," David reminded him.

"Whatever."

"Don't we need to contact an official or something?" Sarah questioned.

"I need a moment to think," Dad answered. "In the meantime, let's bring it into the house."

"James, what kind of dinosaur is it?" Daniel asked as they picked up the bone and headed toward the house.

"I'm not sure," he answered.

A wonderful aroma filled the room as Sarah, James, David, and Daniel set their discovery on the living room floor. Their eyes grew wide with excitement as they realized it was ... "chocolate cake!"

"Yes, and it's almost done. Don't let me forget it."

"We won't," David assured her with a big smile.

"Thanks, Mom!" Sarah said hugging her. "Chocolate is my favorite!"

"Yeah, thanks, Mom," James echoed.

"You should get your dinosaur book," David suggested."

James nodded and raced up the stairs to their room.

James studied the pictures in his book as the family gobbled down their turkey sandwiches. "I think it's a leg bone - maybe it's from a Stegosaurus."

"A what?" Daniel asked.

"It's the kind that walks on four short legs and has spikes down the back."

"Cool!" Sarah said, looking over his shoulder at the picture.

They all jumped when the doorbell rang.

"Who could that be?" Dad wondered.

"I'll go look," James volunteered, swallowing the last bite. He walked over to the door. As he opened it, ten newspaper and TV reporters, with cameras poised ready for action, loomed over him. "Can I help you?" he asked politely.

"There it is!" one reporter yelled, pointing at the bone. With cameras flashing, the reporters pushed their way into the room.

James was almost run over in all the excitement. "Dad, help!"

Dad ran into the room with Mom following right behind him. "Get out!" he yelled, pointing to the door.

Then ....BEEEEEEEEEEEEEEEEEEEEEEEEEEEEEEEEEEEEEEEEEEEEEEEEEEEEEEP!

"Oh, no! My cake! I forgot the cake!" Mom shrieked, running into the kitchen. As she slowly opened the oven door, smoke billowed from the oven into the nearby living room.

Startled first by the alarm and now the smoke, the reporters began to clear the area. Finally, the door was locked, and the shades pulled. The family sat sprawled on the couch.

"What just happened here?" Mom wondered.

"I don't know," Dad replied, wiping the sweat from his brow.

"Mr. Baxter!" James exclaimed. "He was taking out his trash when we found the bone!"

"You're right!" Sarah agreed. "I heard him too!"

James got up and peered out a front window. Sure enough, Mr. Baxter was talking to a TV reporter and pointing toward the backyard. A few minutes later, three white vans pulled up in front of the house. Several police officers – dressed in swat gear – jumped out the back doors. "Dad ..." James began but was interrupted by .... whup ... whup... whup ...whup...WHUP ...WHUP...WHUP ...

WHUP ... WHUP ... WHUP ... WHUP ... WHUP!!!!

"Now what?!" Mom wondered.

Daniel ran over to a window overlooking the backyard. "WOW!!!!" he exclaimed. "It's a ..."

"helicopter from Channel 2 news!" David interrupted, joining him at the window.

"Hey! I was going to say that!" Daniel exclaimed angrily. He gave his brother a push.

"Stop it!" David pushed him back.

"BOYS!" Dad warned.

"The helicopter is hovering over the dig site!" Sarah exclaimed, looking out another window.

"China?" Henry wondered.

"No, Henry," Daniel answered. "We're not digging to China!"

The two-year-old sat on the floor and burst into tears.

"It's okay," Daniel consoled him, but the toddler cried even harder.

There was a loud knock on the door. Dad sighed. "I'll go see who it is."

As he opened the door, a large man with thick black glasses, bushy eyebrows, and a beard pushed his way into the room.

"I'm Mr. Waverly with the Department of Natural Affairs." He showed Dad an important-looking badge. "We're here to take over the dig." He motioned to several men in white uniforms.

"Just a minute!" Dad protested when they picked up the bone. As they headed out the door, a bulldozer plowed through the backyard fence. A backhoe excavator followed right behind.

"Stop!" James yelled from the

window. "That's not how a dig is conducted!"

Chapter 6

There was a loud knock on the door. "Are you okay, Bud?"

James woke with a start. "Yes, Mom."

"Good. Breakfast is ready."

"I'll be right down." He sat up in bed and wiped the sweat from his brow. "That's the last time I eat pizza before bed!" Still a little shaken from the experience, he got up and slowly walked down the stairs.

Sarah greeted him in the kitchen. "James, we're going to finish the fence today! We're getting our puppy in just two days!"

At that moment, the memory of his

dream became all too real. "I don't feel so well," he replied, turning a little pale. "I'm going back to bed."

Sarah watched as he slowly headed up the stairs, walked into his room, and shut the door. "What's wrong with him?" she wondered, wrinkling her forehead.

THE END

Other Books by Patricia Turgeon

The Brave Little Knight and the Dragon

Coming Soon

Mystery at Skull Island

More Than an Orphan

Patricia Turgeon has a passion for making all things beautiful, especially while writing and gardening. She has lived in Minnesota almost her whole life, except for when she traveled the world in her younger years.

The Dig is her second self-published children's book. Visit her website at www.patriciaturgeon.com to learn more about all her other books as they are published and to connect with her on social media.

Sonja Wagenius grew up in a family of artists. Throughout high school, she entered art shows, county fair exhibits, and Yearbook. And later she got her college degree in Art. She continues to sketch daily and participates in open art classes in the community.

Made in the USA
Monee, IL
30 July 2023